FARM LIFE

by **Elizabeth Spurr**

illustrated by
Steve Björkman

Holiday House / New York

For Sherry and Ed Shahan—E. S.

For Michael, whose heart leans
towards farms and ranches—S. B.

Library of Congress Cataloging-in-Publication Data

Spurr, Elizabeth.
Farm life / by Elizabeth Spurr ; illustrated by Steve Björkman.—1st ed.
p. cm.
Summary: Rhymed descriptions of life on a farm introduce basic colors
and the numbers one to ten.
ISBN: 0-8234-1777-8 (hardcover)
1. Counting—Juvenile literature. 2. Colors—Juvenile literature. 3. Farm life—Juvenile literature.
[1. Counting. 2. Colors. 3. Farm life.] I. Björkman, Steve, ill. II. Title.

QA113 .S68 2003
513.211—dc21
[E]   2002027297

RED barn, **RED** barn, what are you keeping?

ONE rumbling tractor ready for reaping,

ONE baler, **ONE** sower,
ONE thresher, **ONE** mower.
This is the farm life—but only a part.

BLUE barn, **BLUE** barn, what are you hiding?
TWO sturdy stallions saddled for riding,

THREE fillies neighing,
FOUR hens a-laying.
This is the farm life—but only a part.

GREEN barn, **GREEN** barn,
what's in your loft?
FIVE bales of hay
with straw piled up soft,

SIX cribs of new corn,
SIX kittens newborn.
This is the farm life—
but only a part.

BROWN barn, **BROWN** barn,
what do you hold?
SEVEN small heifers
escaping the cold,

EIGHT ewes a-feeding,
EIGHT lambs a-bleating.
This is the farm life—but only a part.

GRAY barn, GRAY barn, what do you house?
NINE straw-filled stalls
with NINE sleepy sows,

TEN piglets suckling, Farmer Dan chuckling.
This is the farm life—but only a part.

WHITE house, WHITE house,
open your doors.

Show bright braided rugs on shiny oak floors,

Fresh hot tea steeping, down quilts for sleeping,

A crackling woodstove,
and a family to love.

This is the farm life—the whole and the heart.

GLOSSARY

baler: A machine that ties a field crop, such as hay, after it is gathered

down: Soft fluffy feathers

ewes: Female sheep

fillies: Young female horses

heifers: Young female cattle

loft: The second floor of a barn with an open inside wall

mower: A machine that cuts tall grasses and crops such as oats

piglet: A young pig

reaping: Cutting and gathering a ripened field crop

sow: A full-grown female pig

sower: A machine that scatters or plants seeds

stallion: A full-grown male horse

thresher: A machine that separates seeds from the plants

tractor: A vehicle used to pull a farm machine, such as a plow